# Benny's Had Enough!

*Barbro Lindgren* • *Olof Landström*
Translated by *Elisabeth Kallick Dyssegaard*

R&S
BOOKS

Stockholm   New York   London   Adelaide   Toronto

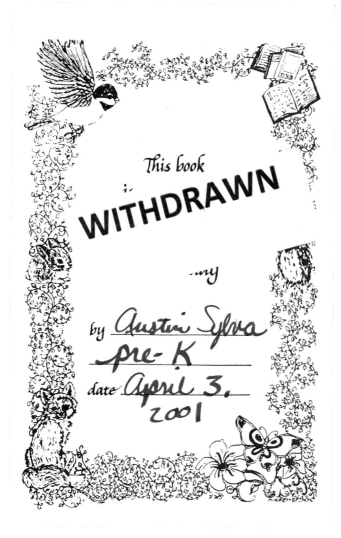

This book

**WITHDRAWN**

...my

by Austin Sylva
pre-K
date April 3,
2001

Rabén & Sjögren Bokförlag, Stockholm
http://www.raben.se
Translation copyright © 1999 by Rabén & Sjögren Bokförlag
All rights reserved
Originally published in Sweden by Rabén & Sjögren under the title *Nämen Benny*
Text copyright © 1998 by Barbro Lindgren
Pictures copyright © 1998 by Olof Landström
Library of Congress catalog card number: 99-70429
Printed in Denmark
First American edition, 1999
Second printing, 2000
ISBN 91-29-64563-8

Benny thinks everything's the pits. His mama is cleaning and cleaning. She is arranging Benny's sticks and potatoes in long rows. But Benny won't let her.

"Oh, Benny," says Benny's mama.

She tries to give Benny a bath in the tub.
But Benny won't let her do that either.
"Oh, Benny," says Benny's mama.

Later, she decides to put Little Piggy in the washing machine.
She thinks he's too dirty. But Little Piggy is not too dirty.
Benny wants him to be much dirtier.

"Oh, Benny," says Benny's mama. But Benny's had enough.
"I can't live here," he cries. He takes Little Piggy and
walks out the door.

But where are they going to live?

Perhaps they can live in a hot-dog stand?
"Can we move into your hot-dog stand?
We don't have a home," Benny says.
"No, you can't," says the hot-dog man.

They keep going. They see a lot of pigs who are sitting in
their cabins and staring at their computer screens.
"Can we move in?" shouts Benny.
But they don't hear him.

Then they meet a dog who seems nice.
"Can we move in with you?"
The dog takes out his cell phone and calls his wife.

"Can Benny and Little Piggy move in with us?"
*"Absolutely not,"* says the dog's wife.
All of a sudden, Benny just has to dig a hole somewhere.

They find a field with red and white flowers next to a small cabin.
Benny starts to dig.

What a great hole. The biggest in town!
"You have to try it, Little Piggy. It's delicious!" shouts Benny.

And so he throws Little Piggy into the hole.
Then a man comes rushing out of the cabin. It's his field.
"Get out of here before I straighten your curly tail!"
screams the man.

Benny is very scared. He sprints away as fast as he can.

He stops in front of the hot-dog stand.
He remembers that Little Piggy is still lying in the hole.
Help! Now he'll have to run back and get him!

He tiptoes the final stretch, so the nasty man won't straighten his curly tail.

When he gets to the hole, it's gone. Someone has put back the dirt. And Little Piggy has been buried. Benny has to dig him up again. But what if the man comes and straightens his curly tail! Life is so hard! If only he had a home and a mama ...

He does, though! And as many sticks and potatoes as he wants.
But just as he's digging the hole again, the man's scary face
pops out the door. Benny throws himself under a bush.

And who is lying under the bush?
Little Piggy!

They are both so happy. Benny takes Little Piggy in his arms and races away.

Now Little Piggy is even dirtier than before. Benny's mama is going to throw him right into the washing machine.

"I'll give you a bath myself," says Benny.
And he dips Little Piggy in a puddle.

Then they move back home.

"Oh, Benny, you've washed Little Piggy!" says Benny's mama.